ESSENTIAL

MORAL STORIES

FOR CHILDREN

ESSENTIAL
MORAL
STORIES
FOR CHILDREN

MOONSTONE

Published in Moonstone
by Rupa Publications India Pvt. Ltd 2023
7/16, Ansari Road, Daryaganj
New Delhi 110002

Sales centres:
Prayagraj Bengaluru Chennai
Hyderabad Jaipur Kathmandu
Kolkata Mumbai

P-ISBN: 978-93-5702-422-8
E-ISBN: 978-93-5702-423-5

First impression 2023

10 9 8 7 6 5 4 3 2 1

Printed in India

CONTENTS

The
Cap Seller

A cap seller visited many cities with his big bag of caps. They were loved by all because of their quality.

One day, the seller was taking a nap under a tree. He kept his bag beside him, and covered his face to get some shade.

The tree he slept beneath was home to some monkeys, who climbed down and imitated his snoring while he remained fast asleep.

13

One of them opened the seller's bag. The others toppled the entire bag and wore his caps.

The moment the seller woke up, all the monkeys hid. He saw his caps all over the ground and the empty bag.

The seller shouted, "Who took my caps?" Two monkeys climbed down and started teasing him.

The monkeys started imitating him,
and so he threw his cap. Both
the monkeys threw their caps too.
The seller quickly picked them
up and went on his way.

The Foolish
Monkey

Every year, the animals and birds started repairing their homes to prepare for the onset of rain.

The rains were accompanied by heavy lightning and loud thunder. All the animals and birds remained inside their cosy homes.

One day, a monkey climbed on the tree where the birds had settled. The monkey was drenched and desperately needed shelter.

The leaves were not big enough to protect the monkey. The poor monkey had nowhere to go and got wet in the rain.

The Greedy Hen

GRAINS

41

"Look! There is a big pot behind the bushes," said the yellow hen and they peeked inside the pot.

49

GRAINS

The Intelligent
Lamb

One day, a little lamb strayed away from its flock while a wolf was watching it. Its mouth started watering as it looked at the lamb.

The lamb was quick-witted and said, "I know you'll devour me soon but I have a last wish. My friends told me that you sing very well."

61

"Your voice is extremely melodious! I wish you could keep singing for me." The wolf felt ecstatic. It started singing again, at the top of its voice.

The shepherd heard the wolf singing and found the missing lamb. He attacked the wolf from behind with his stick. The sheep got together and sprang on the wolf too.

The wolf ran away while the lamb rushed to its flock.

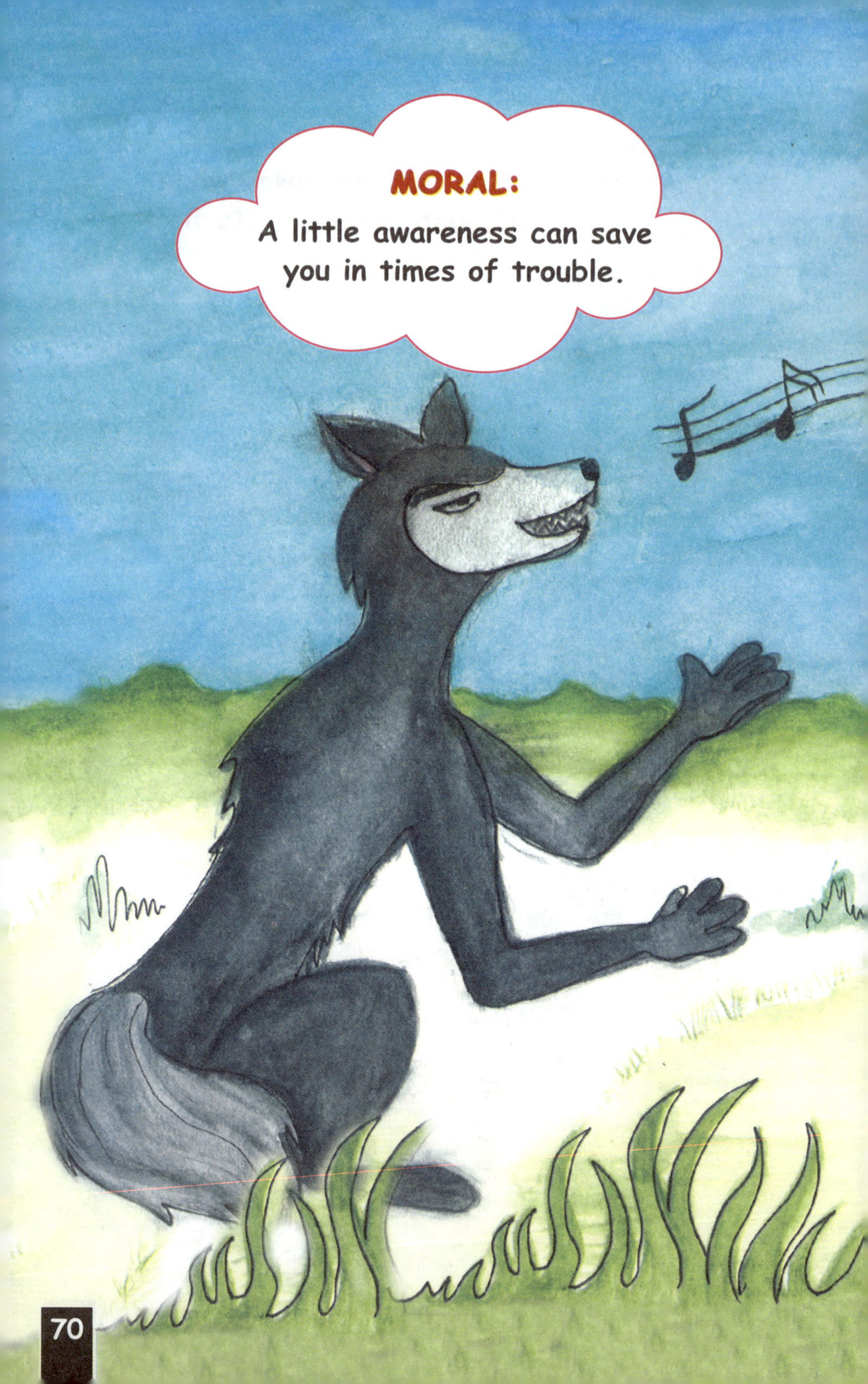
MORAL:
A little awareness can save you in times of trouble.

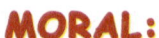

The Mice and the Cat

The mouse family settled in the granary and kept munching more and more grain each day.

The mice got together. "None of us will be left alive if this situation remains. The cat is fast and silent; we can't fight individually," the eldest mouse commented.

MORAL:

Some suggestions can be excellent, but they might not always be realistic.

The Soup Party

One day, the fox offered to make soup for them. However, as it tasted the soup, it couldn't stop eating it.

The stork went home with an empty stomach. It knew that the fox had done this deliberately and decided to turn the tables.

The Sparrow
and the
Kingfisher

"Why can we not catch fish?" the sparrow asked its friend. "Because we are different and cannot dive in the river," its friend explained.

The little sparrow was not convinced. "They are all scared of water, but I am not," it thought.

It decided to fly up in the air and dive in the water just like the kingfisher.

It came down at high speed but lost control in the air. **Splash!** It fell into the river and injured one of its wings.

115

For many days, the little sparrow could not fly with its friends. It had to sit on the tree, all bandaged up.

The Stupid
Jackal

121

They once decided to cross the river. The jackal sat on the camel's back and travelled for the exploration.

129

As they were running, the camel walked into the deeper waters. "I will drown if you go any further!" the jackal said.

The Wise Mule

A mule used to live with a farmer. It couldn't do much due to old age and wasted its time roaming the farm.

137

One day, the mule fell into the farm's well. It was trying to jump out of the well but was unable to. The farmer saw its struggle and called over his friends.

138

As his friends started digging up mud and filling the well, the mule let out a cry. It was scared of getting buried.

The mule thought it would
be able to get out of the
well after a few more buckets
of mud.

149

The Grapes are Sour

157

Eventually, the fox grew tired and gave up. It went away saying, "I do not want these grapes. These grapes are sour!"